WANDA THE WILOPENT

a children's story
by
JOANNE CUCINELLO

with illustrations by
RACHAEL MAHAFFEY

Joanne Cucinello

ISBN: 1-4196-8907-X
ISBN-13: 9781419689079
Library of Congress Control Number: 2008900725

Visit www.booksurge.com to order additional copies.

This book is dedicated to my loving husband Al and my five wonderful children, Cherylyn, Christine, Lisa, Brendan and Paul whose encouragement and persistence nudged me on to keep writing and follow my dream and to my precious grandchildren who tiptoe through all my inspirations...

It was a gray and rainy day in the Toad King's forest. Big droplets of rain were bouncing off the tops of toadstools and all through the forest, the bumpy squeaks of the Wilopents echoed down in the moss.

Here and there, they scrambled in their usual clusters, bumping and squeaking, till they finally found a toadstool large enough to protect them and keep them dry.

It was not fun for Wilopents on rainy days, and I'll tell you why. If a little Wilopent gets too wet, its bumps start to grow wild and crazy and then all the other Wilopents have to pile on top of him till he dries and the crazy bumps go down. This is a very noisy predicament and not much fun for the one on the bottom! And besides, a wet Wilopent is a scary looking thing you wouldn't want to see.

The Wilopents aren't the only ones in the Toad King's forest.

Tiny wing-flutters can be heard in-between the rain drops some days, the sounds of the Pygmy Fairies, as they flutter and giggle, sprinkling fairy dust everywhere. It's a magical place, to be sure, in the Toad King's forest, and this is where the story of Wanda the Wilopent begins.

Little Wanda was not just an ordinary Wilopent. Yes, she was bumpy and lumpy just like the rest, but there was something very different about her, right from the start. Wanda wanted to be a Fairy.

Now, everyone knows that Wilopents can never be Fairies, just as Fairies can never be Wilopents. But that didn't matter much to Wanda. She was sure, if she tried hard enough, she could find a way to be one.

Something else was different about Wanda. I'm sure you've heard that Wilopents always wobble from place to place in clusters. They stick together like glue. That was, except for Wanda. Even when she was a little baby, Wanda always wobbled behind the rest and liked to sit under her own toadstool when it rained.

Some of the Wilopents thought she was snooty and used to stick out their furry tongues at her. "Na, Na"!! But Wanda didn't mind. She liked to be different and besides, she hated being squashed in a Wilopent clump.

It was on one of those rainy days, when she was alone under her toadstool, that an adorable Pygmy Fairy fluttered by to take a peek. "Why aren't you over there with the others?" she asked. Wanda replied, "Because I'm not **like** the others. That's why!"

The Fairy fluttered and giggled, "Oh, yes, you are! Why, you're bumpy and lumpy just like the rest. Stick out your tongue. I'll bet it's furry too."

"So what!" cried Wanda. "You can't see where I'm different. It's on the inside."

"Oh my" said the Fairy, flipping her tiny wings and tumbling over with joy, "That's wonderful! You know, I'm different too."

"Really?" asked Wanda. "What makes you different? You have wings and cute pony tails. You flutter and giggle and sprinkle that silly dust all over, just like the others . . . which, by the way, makes me sneeze! *Achoo!* So why are you different?"

"I guess I'm different . . . because I've fallen in love . . . with the Toad King."

"Oh my goodness," gasped Wanda, "the horrible Toad King?"

"He's not **really** horrible. It's just his loud "GRIBBET!!" that scares everyone in the forest, but that's why he's the King.

I fell in love when I heard his sad beautiful song float through the trees one night, when the moon was blue.

It wasn't a *gribbett* . . . it was a **melody**. Fairies don't have melodies. We only have fairy dust and dreams."

"I have dreams too!" said Wanda. "I dream that I can be a fairy, just like you, and fly in the moonlight, adorable and sparkly. I dream that I can be a different kind of Wilopent.

Do you think that's possible, Fairy?"

"Fairies think **anything** is possible . . . if you want it bad enough!".

Well now, what do you think happened to these two little forest creatures who dared to dream of being different?

Let's go on with the story:

Wanda and Fairy both knew there was magic hidden in the Toad King's forest, but there was also danger for those who traveled alone. The little Wilopent became very sad that night and tried with all her might to think of a way to make her dream come true. Fairy was busy dusting flowers in the moonlight and wiping away her tears, when suddenly Wanda's tiny brain went "POP!!"

"I know what to do now, Fairy. I will wobble through the forest and listen for the Toad King's song. I will follow his melody and find my way to his Great Toad Hut, and when I do, I will ask him to make my dream come true, for I can't stay a Wilopent forever. . . I want to fly like you."

"You're very brave, little Wilopent. I want to go with you but I know I can never face the Toad King and bare my heart. He is a Toad and I'm a Fairy and I can only love him in my dreams. Be careful now, and may all your dreams come true."

And that was the night that changed Wanda the Wilopent's life forever. Into the deep dark forest she wobbled, through mud and marshes, brush and thickets. The sound of the night owls chilled her to the bone, but there in the distance she heard the lovely sad song of the Toad King, floating gently through the whispering trees.

"Why am I so sad?" she thought. "There is no sound sadder than the lonely song of the Toad King. He must be lonelier than the Moon up there in the dark night sky."

On and on she wobbled, full of scratches and leaves and broken twigs that stuck to her lumpy bumps, but nothing stopped her. Wanda followed the melody through the forest with only her heart to guide her.

And then it happened. She saw the magical Toad King, sitting on his lonely throne deep in the moonlit forest. But somehow, he did not look very magical. Wanda stood behind a droopy willow tree, watching sadly. She saw that something was very wrong. Tears were falling from his big green eyes like jaded crystals. Everything inside Wanda was telling her to wobble away as fast as she could, but instead, the little Wilopent stirred up all her courage and came out of the thicket.

Wanda stood there in the pale moonlight and bashfully smiled her Wilopent smile. Then she stuck out her furry tongue and tried to make the Toad King laugh, but he didn't. He just lifted his head and dried his sad green eyes. Wanda looked again and sighed, "Oh my!" You truly are the Toad King. What a beautiful crown you have, dear Sir."

The King wondered who this little creature might be. Wanda was silent. She just smiled again and stuck out her tongue. This time the Toad King almost laughed.

"Who are you, little lump? And why have you wandered so deep in the forest?"

"I am Wanda the Wilopent" she answered, "a creature in your kingdom, Great King. I have come all this way to find you because I know you are magical and can make my dream come true. But I see that your heart is broken and it was selfish of me to come."

"You are very brave to travel the dark night alone." said the King. "Poor creature, I have no magic to make your dream come true. My power was stolen long ago."

"But Sir, you ARE powerful!" cried Wanda. "You are the King of the Forest. Why every creature hears your loud and powerful "GRIBBET!" and shudders."

"Once I was strong and powerful; once my magic was real" he said sadly.

Wanda stood in the moss before the sad green King and listened now with all her heart.

"Don't you see I am chained to this throne?"

Wanda looked down at the Toad Kings legs and saw the strong silver chains that held him down.

"I sing in the moonlight, hoping someone will hear my lonely heart and set me free. But you are the only creature who's come and you can not help me, little one. You're too small. I am bound by these chains forever."

The Frog King went on to tell Wanda how he was captured by an evil Wart from the dark muddy swamp one night and chained to his throne, never to leap free again, with chains too strong to break and not a creature strong enough to even try.

It was then that everything changed inside of Wanda. She stopped thinking about her dream of being a fairy and she started thinking about how to save the King.

Wilopents are very small when it's nice and sunny and there's not a raindrop in sight, but not when it rains!

Wanda turned to the sad King and said," I know how to set you free!"

"Oh little one, not a creature in the forest is strong enough to break these chains, and surely not one as small as you." He hung his head and sighed, "You must go back to your home now, where you'll be safe. "See," he pointed to the sky, "a storm is coming and the clouds are dark and full of rain and . . . ."

"Rain?" cried Wanda, before he could finish. "Oh, that's wonderful!!!!! "Rain. . . LOTS OF RAIN! Yippee!!!

Then she smiled and stuck out her furry tongue shouting, as a crash of thunder shook the sky, "You don't understand, Good King, I am a Wilopent . . . and we Wilopents HATE the rain!" With that, Wanda scurried off toward home through the bushes, wobbling and squeaking.

The Toad King scratched his head in disbelief as Wanda shouted, "I'll be back, just wait and see. Soon you'll be free!!"

Wanda began her journey home in the dark. She tried to remember the way she came, but suddenly the bushes and trees seemed thicker and thicker around her and she went deeper and deeper into the forest. Just when it seemed the little Wilopent was lost, she saw a sparkly light shining in the distance. Wanda thought, "That looks like fairy dust!" And guess what? She was right!

Wanda wobbled as fast as she could, following the sparkly light and before she knew it, "Smack!" she bumped right into her . . . the tiny Pygmy Fairy, sprinkling her fairy dust and giggling her fairy giggle. The little Wilopent was home.

"You saved me, Fairy. Oh, thank you!"

"How's that?" asked Fairy.

"With the light from your fairy dust and you know what?" Wanda stopped herself just then, leaned over and whispered in the fairy's ear, "That's just what we need to save the King."

"Save the King!" whispered back Fairy. "How is that possible?"

Well, you know, they say that even the trees have ears in the forest, so Wanda had to be very quiet about her wonderful idea.

Wanda drew close to the fairy and whispered her plan and Fairy fluttered and tumbled with glee at the thought that she could help free the Toad King. After all, Fairy loved him.

Now, the hardest part was yet to come, to convince all the Wilopents to help her.

Wanda called to the Wilopents, "Come out, come out from your toadstools."

One by one they shouted, "No!" to Wanda.

The oldest Wilopent came out of the cluster, which was very hard to do, and said, "Don't you see the dark rain clouds ready to pour on us, Wanda?" And her mother came forward too saying, "And by the way, where have you been all night, young lady?" Wanda wobbled forward and whispered in their ears, "I've been to see the Toad King".

"Uh!" gasped her mother.

"You what?" asked the old Wilopent.

"I've been to see the King of the Forest."

"Wanda, why would you do such a dangerous thing? He could have eaten you up for his dinner!"

"No, no", giggled Wanda. "He didn't even know we were here in his kingdom . . . and that's because we're always hiding under toadstools. But NOW he knows, because the Wilopents are going to save him!!"

Wanda's little brother wriggled out from the cluster, all of a sudden feeling very brave, and asked in his tiny voice, "Why do we have to save the great King?"

And with that, Wanda began to quietly whisper the story of the Toad King's capture and the horrible chains and his big green crystal tears. As she spoke, one by one, the Wilopents wriggled out of their clusters and came to listen to Wanda's story and how they all could save him.

"This is a very scary plan you have" said her brother.

"I know it's scary" Wanda whispered, "but we can do it!"

The thunder started to shake the sky again and a bolt of lightening crackled. "Oh, oh . . . I don't know about this" said another Wilopent trying to run and hide. "Listen", cried Wanda," we have to be brave. We can do something WONDERFUL. We can save our King!!"

And as she was speaking, plop, plop, the raindrops started to fall. Wanda's lumpy bumps started popping up. Her little brother's lumpy bumps started to pop. And before they knew it, all the Wilopents were starting to grow.

"Come on" said Wanda, and now she shouted as loud as her little voice could shout. "It's now or never. CHARGE!!!!!!!"

Can you imagine the sight of the Wilopents, charging through the forest, getting wetter and wetter and BIGGER AND BIGGER, LUMPIER AND BUMPIER? Why, soon they looked like GIANTS. They were even knocking down trees!!

And there at the head of them all was Wanda, heart pounding and waving the Wilopent flag. Fairy led the way in the stormy dark night and even in the storm, her sparkly light never went out.

"Come on" yelled Wanda, in her now very big voice, "we're almost there!"

Up ahead was the thicket of the Toad King. Wanda said to Fairy, "You go ahead Fairy and tell the King not to be afraid . . . the Wilopents are coming!!!!"

Now it was Fairy's turn to be the brave one. She flew ahead, saying over and over to herself, "I'm not afraid, I'm not afraid". But she was afraid . . . to finally come face to face with the King.

The thunder was crashing all around her, and here and there the lightening lit up the sky. Just as she was almost there, a bolt of lightening lit up the sky above thicket and she saw him, the King that she loved.

"Oh my King" she thought, and she mustered up all her courage and flew to his throne. The Toad Kings head was bending low and Fairy could see his great sadness.

"Sir" she whispered as she flew right up to his face, her little wings fluttering and her fairy dust sparkling, "the Wilopents are coming through the forest and soon they will break your chains and set you free." The King shook his head saying, "Oh no, little Wanda, out in this terrible storm. I sent her away to be safe."

"Dear King" fluttered Fairy, "Wanda isn't small TODAY!"

And just as she said that, a terrible noise came rumbling into the thicket, the loudest squeaking and bumping the forest ever knew. The King lifted his head and there they were, the Giant Wilopents.

"Don't be afraid, Sir" giggled Fairy, "it's only Wanda and the Wilopents. Close your eyes, they're pretty scary, all yucky and wet, but now they can break your chains. You'll see in a snap. This was Wanda's very own plan."

"I can't believe it", the King said, shaking his head in wonder.

"CHARGE!!" roared Wanda and all the Wilopents piled in a clump and tugged and pulled and "CRACK!!" went the chains. The King was free!!

And then something magical happened. It used to happen every morning long ago deep in the forest, when the King was a happy king.

Not a sound could be heard again now. Even the tiniest ant was still and quiet, everything was hushed. The rain stopped still in the air, the dark clouds floated away. Drooping leaves of the willow trees lifted up their branches and a beautiful lark began to sing. The warm rays of the morning sun streamed through the trees and the Toad King smiled. He smiled and smiled and smiled some more and then he stood on his magic throne. With a loud and happy "Grrribbet!" he called to all the creatures of the forest, "Gribbet, gribbet, gribbet! "Wake up, wake up, it's a brand new day and you're king is happy again."

As the sun grew warmer, Wanda and the Wilopents shrunk and shrunk till they were dry and tiny once more. Then they stuck out their furry tongues all together to make the green King laugh.

Well, he laughed and he laughed, and then spread out his arms and looked down at Wanda sitting shyly on the grass.

And that's when the magic happened. The Toad King reached out his golden wand and tapped little Wanda on her head. "You, little Wanda, are the bravest creature in the forest. I will grant your wish this day. Tell me what it is."

Wanda thought for a moment and then she said to the King, "Your Majesty, I wish that I had golden pigtails just like Fairy"

"Golden pigtails, is that all?"

Fairy tumbled over and whispered in Wanda's ear "What about the wings?"

"I don't need wings anymore, Fairy. I'm a Wilopent and Wilopents don't need to fly." Wanda had grown up inside that night she saved the King.

Toad King tapped Wanda's head again and *Poof* there were golden pigtails.

Then he turned to Fairy, "Now I remember you, sweet Fairy, I remember your light and how I could see you sparkle through the trees when I was all alone. You gave me hope. For this you will fly by my side forever."

Then he turned to all the Wilopents and said,

"It is true that Wilopents don't need to fly, but that is because from this day forward you will ride on my back and go wherever I go. You are all my dearest and bravest friends."

And so dear children, this is the end of our story, but it's only the beginning of Wanda the Wilopent's new life. So if ever you come into the forest one day, and I'm sure you will, you may be lucky enough to see the Toad King hopping by with little bumps on his back. And if you're really quiet you will hear them squeaking with joy, because they aren't really bumps, you know, it's just Wanda and the Wilopents.

1549536